# Mamá's Birthday Surprise

# Mamá's Birthday Surprise

Elizabeth Spurr
Illustrated by Felipe Dávalos

Hyperion Books for Children
New York

For my siblings: Ted, Kathy, and Tom
—E. S.

Text © 1996 by Elizabeth Spurr.
Illustrations © 1996 by Felipe Dávalos.

Printed in the United States of America.

First Edition
1 3 5 7 9 10 8 6 4 2

This book is set in 13-point Leawood.
Designed by Lara S. Demberg.

Library of Congress Cataloging-in-Publication Data
Spurr, Elizabeth.
    Mamá's Birthday Surprise / Elizabeth Spurr ; illustrated
by Felipe Dávalos. — 1st ed.
       p.        cm.
    Summary: Three children grow up with their hardworking mother's
stories about her rich uncle back in Mexico, but when they save
money for a visit, they learn a surprising truth.
    ISBN 0-7868-0265-0 (trade)—ISBN 0-7868-1124-2 (pbk.)
    1. Mexican Americans—Juvenile fiction. [1. Mexican Americans—
Fiction. 2. Family life—Fiction. 3. Uncles—Fiction.]
I. Dávalos, Felipe, ill.  II. Title.
PZ7.S7695Mam        1996
[Fic]—dc20                                      95-53842

# CONTENTS

# ONE
# MAMÁ'S STORIES

"Pepe, careful! Be careful of *Tío* César."

From the time I was tall enough to reach the mantel, it was my job to dust the living room. After warning me, Mamá pretended not to watch as I fluffed the feather duster across the carved gilded frame.

The smiling photo of Uncle César, in his embroidered vest and large *sombrero*, stood in the place of honor beside of a small wooden statue of *la Virgen de Guadalupe*. He was our family's hero, its *patrón*.

After dusting, I stepped onto the footstool and put a small vase of our garden flowers in front of the Virgin. Mamá nudged it a little to the right, closer to the photo.

"In Guadalajara, *Tío* is also revered as a saint." While I finished my work she would relate one of her many stories about the good deeds of her rich uncle.

"Ah, yes. He was very rich. His *hacienda* in Guadalajara had seven chimneys and dozens of *cuartos* and *baños*. Imagine, all those bedrooms and baths!"

Our home in Glendale was neat but crowded, with only two small bedrooms and one bathroom for the four of us. Mamá often gazed at the picture of Uncle and his stately hacienda. Maybe she was wondering, as we did, why she had ever left her carefree life in Mexico.

Every evening after dinner, Pablo, Rosa, and I did the dishes. Because I was the youngest, I could only dry the things that wouldn't break: the knives and forks, the pots and pans. While we worked, Mamá would sit at the kitchen table with her *café con leche* and tell more stories about life with Uncle César. We'd heard them all a hundred times, but sometimes she'd add new details, or leave something out. Pablo, who was the oldest, loved to catch her.

"Uncle had more than two hundred horses and a thousand head of cattle."

"One hundred horses," said Pablo.

"Right, one hundred horses."

"But, Mamá, why do you change things?" asked Rosa.

"To make sure you are listening, *querida*."

Tío César's hacienda sat on a hill, named *Montaña de Oro*—the mountain of gold—because of its golden grain. Later real gold was discovered on Uncle César's lands. He became the richest man in the village, perhaps in the whole province, but he never forgot the poor.

Mamá had gone to live with Tío César when she lost her parents in a great earthquake. Tío was very kind to her.

He bought necklaces of polished stones, dresses with lace ruffles, and shoes trimmed in real silver. He gave her singing, dancing, and guitar lessons and tutoring in English.

On each of her birthdays, he invited the whole village to her *fiesta de cumpleaños*. The lawns and gardens were strung with flickering lanterns and strolling *mariachis* played and sang into the night.

"You left out the part about the dolls," said Rosa.

Mamá looked up at the ceiling. "Oh yes, *las muñecas*. Every year Tío gave me a doll with a real china face, dressed in a costume from some far-away country. The dolls were all handmade, and much too fancy to play with. I kept them on a shelf in my bedroom, a prized collection."

Rosa smiled, satisfied.

When Mamá was sixteen, her uncle gave a splendid celebration for her confirmation into the church. She wore a white lace gown and a crown of gardenias. Guillermo, a famous painter, came to do her portrait.

After that, young men were allowed to call. Many came to serenade her, but their music was wasted on the night air until our papá came along.

He was one of her guitar teachers, on vacation from the university. With his speakers and synthesizer blaring, "I Want to Hold Your Hand," he soon had the whole village dancing. "And my heart, as well," said Mamá.

• • •

Uncle César gave Mamá a magnificent wedding with twelve bridesmaids, but he scowled through the two days of feasting. And when a coach and white horses drove the bride and groom away, Tío stood with folded arms and would not wave good-bye.

"He was upset," Mamá explained. "You see, your papá was a *gringo*, from the USA."

"I like the part about the gun," said Pablo.

"When did I tell you about the gun?"

"Not for a long time. Maybe you've forgotten."

Mamá paused for a moment. "*Sí*, the gun. He whipped the pistol from his holster and fired toward the carriage. The horses shied and galloped off with us."

This part scared me. "Was anyone hurt?"

"Oh, no, Pepe. Your tío would not harm anyone."

"Then why did he shoot?"

"Could be he was just joking." She fingered the gold cross at her throat. "Or perhaps he was afraid Papá would take me away forever."

"Don't worry," Pablo whispered to me. "It's just a story."

Mamá always told her stories with lots of poses and gestures, with shouts, and sometimes even tears.

"We came to California shortly before Pablo was born. Your father got a good job with a radio station in Los Angeles. He was a fine *deesk* jockey." She always pronouced her *i*'s like *e*'s.

"We bought this house brand-new. When Rosa came along, then Pepe, our family was very happy. We had plans to build on a second story. . . ."

At this point Mamá would stop and cover her eyes. We waited through her silence. "Papá was killed in a car crash on New Year's Eve. When you, Pepe, were only a baby."

I knew my father only as the handsome man in the wedding photo Mamá kept beside her bed.

"When Papá brought me to the States," said

Mamá, "Uncle César became very angry. He became even more angry when, after Papá's death, I would not return with you to Mexico.

"But do not fear, *queridos*," she assured us. "Tío César loves us dearly. He will always take care of his family. Ah yes. If we were ever in need, I would only have to say the word. He would send a bushel basket full of pesos."

But somehow, Mamá never said the word.

After Papá's death, Mamá's life was not easy. The insurance money soon dwindled. Mamá got a job in an office. Three evenings a week she went to college to earn a teaching degree.

On those nights our neighbor Mrs. Brady came to look after us. She was fat and drank a lot of water and would not let us talk during dinner. We hated staying with Mrs. Brady and sometimes played tricks on her. Like putting bubble gum on the seat of her rocker. Or sneaking salt into her water glass.

Coming home after class, Mamá would drop into her flowered armchair and sigh, "I'm so tired!"

Then she'd pick up her books to study.

"Poor Mamá," said Rosa. "Why do you work so hard? Why don't we go home to Uncle César?"

Mamá shook her head. "Home," she said, "is here in the *Estados Unidos*. This is the land of opportunity. And *we* are citizens."

# TWO
## MAMÁ'S LETTERS

Every Sunday before Mass, Mamá lit a candle for Uncle César. When she got home from church, she wrote him a long letter, which she tucked into her purse to mail on Monday.

Uncle César never wrote back. Mamá made many excuses. "This is the time of the harvest." "Maybe he is busy with the roundup." "Now it is time for the planting."

We questioned her: "Mamá, is he still angry?"

"Of course not."

"Are you sure?"

"Well, perhaps. All the more reason for me to write."

She always read us what she wrote. "Pepe has

9

made his First Communion." "Pablo is on the ninth-grade honor roll." "My sweet peas are blooming all over the garden wall."

She never relayed any bad news. When Rosa sliced her thumb with the butcher knife, needing six stitches, Mamá wrote, "Rosa is learning to cook."

Mamá also never told her uncle that she had to work. Her first job was receptionist for Mr. Hoffman, who owned an insurance agency. His office was over the health-food store just a short walk from our home. Mr. Hoffman had recently lost his wife, so Mamá invited him to dinner on holidays.

Rosa used to tease Mamá, "I think Mr. Hoffman likes you."

Mamá would pretend not to hear.

"Mr. H wants to be Mamá's boyfriend."

Mamá shushed her with a clucking noise. "I'm too busy for such things." She smiled and looked away. "Besides, your papá is still *mi novio*."

At Christmas, Mr. Hoffman would bring us a turkey and gifts. One year he gave Mamá a fancy silver comb for her hair, but she never wore it. She kept it wrapped in the silk scarf he had given her the year before.

"I am saving these gifts for our visit to Uncle César," she said. "Then I will want to look *muy hermosa*." But Mamá, with her dark, shadowy eyes and wide smile, did not need scarves or combs to make her beautiful.

## THREE
# SAVING FOR THE VISIT

A painted piggy bank named *Jamón* stood on top of the refrigerator. Jamón was like a member of the family. When we earned money doing odd jobs, or found pennies and nickels on the sidewalk, we fed the change to Jamón. With the money saved in the pig, one day Mamá would take us to visit Uncle César.

Mr. Hoffman paid Mamá every Friday. On Saturday morning we all carried baskets to the open-air market, held in the parking lot of the Super-Rite. Mamá bought dried beans and fresh vegetables, along with *chilis* and *tomatillos* for *salsa*.

Before any purchase, she walked past all the stalls to make sure she got the best price. "Señor Valdez

has onions four for a dollar," she said to the vendor, who then would drop an extra one in her sack.

"What do you mean, two dollars for tomatoes?" she said to another. "I will grow my own."

"You'd better taste these first," said the farmer. He gave her a free sample, which she pocketed with a *"gracias."*

We nibbled fresh fruit in the shade of a laurel tree while Mamá wheeled a cart inside the Super-Rite to select her groceries. She came out smiling—"Good bargains today"—and gave us the sacks to carry home.

While we spread the groceries on the kitchen table, Mamá asked us what we would like for our special dinner. Dinner on Saturday was always like a *fiesta*. Mamá spent the afternoon cooking dishes she had learned from Miguel, the chef who worked for Uncle César.

"Ah, you should see Uncle's kitchen," she said. "As big as this whole house. With a great wood-stove of cast iron, and huge metal pots hanging from a ceiling rack." She would hold out her arms

15

to show us their size. "I would have to stand on a chair to stir the soup."

"But, Mamá," said Rosa. "Why did the cook use such large pots? There were only the two of you."

"You forget, we had many household servants to feed. Field-workers, too." Mamá looked hurt, as she sometimes did when we questioned her stories.

Rosa unpacked the cornmeal. "Mamá, may we have *tamales* tonight?"

"No, it's my turn." Pablo held up the package of chicken. "Let's have *arroz con pollo*."

"You always get to choose," whined Rosa.

When I asked for *carne asada*, Mamá sighed, "Sorry, Pepe, steak is too expensive."

She put her chin in her hands and pretended to consider our requests. "Tonight I'll make Uncle César's favorite." She gave the dish a fancy Mexican name, "*Comida del Rey*." Most likely it would turn out to be something cheap, like *enchiladas* or *burritos de frijoles*, fancied-up beans with cheese.

On Saturday evenings we ate by candlelight. Mamá taught us the table manners she had learned in Uncle César's elegant dining hall, which we would enjoy someday. "Rosa, sit tall." "Pablo, keep your napkin in your lap." "Pepe, your fork! Please use your other hand."

At this special meal we had to keep our forks in our left hands, as they do in Mexico. We were allowed to speak only in Spanish; Mamá did not want us to forget our Mexican heritage.

After we had put the groceries away and filed the unused cents-off coupons in the kitchen drawer, Mamá dropped the change from her purse into the pig. She held Jamón in her hands and shook him. "Ah, the pig is getting fat. Uncle César would be pleased."

She patted the pig's sides. "Even when he became wealthy, your uncle was thrifty with his *dinero*. Generous, but still thrifty. That is how he got rich."

When the pig was full, she would empty the coins into a canvas bag, stamped AMERICAN SAVINGS BANK. Mamá always beamed with pride when she poured money into that sack.

# FOUR
# A Lean Christmas

One evening Mamá came home with tears in her eyes. "Mr. Hoffman is closing his office. He is relocating his business to Palm Springs."

She grabbed a dish towel and began to cry. "I will have no work."

"No job?" said Pablo.

"No money?" I asked.

"No trip to Mexico," said Rosa. She joined Mamá in her sobs.

"Why don't we write to Uncle César?" said Pablo. "He probably lights his cigars with pesos."

Mamá smiled faintly and wiped her eyes. "But yes, of course. I'll write Tío tomorrow." She gathered us into her arms. "Now let's pop some corn."

She seemed cheerful when we kissed her *buenas noches* but I heard her crying in the night.

The next morning Mamá wrote to Uncle César. She folded the letter into her purse. "Don't worry. Money will come soon."

Mamá's job lasted only two more weeks. But by Thanksgiving eve, her last workday, the money had not arrived. Mamá made excuses. "Maybe Uncle César is busy with the planting."

"But, Mamá," said Rosa. "He would not sow in the fall."

"With the harvest, then. That's it, the harvest. Do not worry, *hijos*, the money will come soon."

"Why don't you call him?" asked Pablo.

"I do not have his number," she said. "A man of his importance is not listed in the directory."

Pablo looked at Rosa and me, then rolled his eyes and whistled a tune, as he sometimes did when Mamá made excuses.

By Christmastime no money had appeared. Mamá said we must spend nothing on gifts.

Rosa pouted, "What is Christmas for?"

"More than giving and receiving," said Mamá. "*Navidad* is a time for loving."

"Sure thing," said Pablo. "Did your loving uncle César teach you that?" He jammed his hands in his pockets and stormed off.

Mamá's answer didn't satisfy Rosa, either. The next afternoon she pulled an old torn sheet from the closet. "Mamá didn't say we couldn't *give*. She said we could not *spend*."

She cut the sheet in the shape of Mamá's dining table and began fringing the edges. Then she cut smaller squares for napkins and showed Pablo and me how to fringe.

"This is girls' work," Pablo grumbled, but kept working.

A few days later, when Mamá was at night class, Rosa dyed all the squares in leftover coffee, then dried and ironed them. "Look," she said proudly. "Better than the tablecloths in the department store."

With our door closed, Pablo and I strung necklaces of macaroni for Rosa. We dyed them with food coloring, which left pink and green stains on our sheets. We had to keep our beds made so Mamá wouldn't see.

Two weeks before Christmas we brought out our old Nativity scene. We sang "*Las Posadas*" as we placed Mary and Joseph by the crib. The angel was missing a wing.

I dropped Baby Jesus and chipped his ear. "Now look what you've done." Pablo pinched my ear. "See how it feels, little brother?"

I squinted, trying not to cry.

"Pablo, apologize!" Rosa scolded. She picked up the figure. "Never mind, Pepe. I can patch the Infant with paste. Remember, we don't bring out the *Bebé* until Christmas Eve."

We put votive lights and pine branches in front of the crib. Mamá came home just as we finished. "Ah, muy hermosa. See how pretty?"

"Pretty bare," said Pablo. "Mamá, no matter what you say, we need a tree!"

On Christmas Eve, Pablo and I went to the tree lot after it had closed. We found several unwanted

firs in the Dumpster and took the largest one home.

"Ah, so tall!" said Mamá.

For sure, it was much larger than any tree we'd had before. There would not be nearly enough ornaments.

"Ornaments are no problem," said Rosa. "I'll show you."

For hours we cut colored magazine pages into star and angel shapes, then wrapped the tree in paper chains and popcorn.

"Enough, *hijos*," said Mamá. "It is time for *la Misa del Gallo*."*

Before leaving for Midnight Mass, we stood back and stared at the fully decorated tree. It was our most beautiful ever.

In the morning, there were several gifts under the tree. Mamá's eyes sparkled when she saw the tablecloth. She laid it on the table and brought out her best dishes to serve our favorite coffee cake and hot chocolate. "I am *muy feliz*," she said. "This gift is from your hearts."

*The Rooster's Mass, so named because the cock is expected to crow and announce the birth of the child

After breakfast we opened more gifts. Rosa had made Pablo and me a *piñata* from an oatmeal box and shredded Sunday comics. It was a funny-looking rabbit with droopy ears, filled with bags of homemade powdered sugar cookies and cactus candy.

Then Mamá, her face beaming, presented us with a large carton in silver wrapping. In it was a new guitar, inlaid with mother-of-pearl.

"But, Mamá," said Rosa. "We were not supposed to spend money."

Mamá's eyes shone. "The guitar is a gift to me. I have a new job. In a music store!"

Mamá had a strong, clear voice. The store had given her the guitar so she could practice songs she had learned in Mexico. She would demonstrate the instruments and sing near the store entrance to draw customers in from the mall. Afternoons she would work in the office, assisting Mrs. Salmacia, the owner, with letters and bookkeeping.

"A new job for Mamá," said Pablo. "That's the best gift of all!"

Three tissue-wrapped packages remained under the tree. Mamá handed one to each of us. From an old skirt she had made three ruffled shirts, the kind worn on special days in Mexico.

"Mamá," said Rosa, "you made these for our visit to Uncle César!"

Mamá smiled but did not answer.

Pablo threw down his new shirt. "Why should we visit Uncle César? What kind of tío is he? Some patrón! Why didn't he send money when we needed it?"

Mamá lowered her eyes. "Because I did not ask him."

"But, Mamá, you said . . ."

"I said only that I would write him. I did not say I would ask for money. And isn't it better that I didn't? We did not need it. This was our best Navidad ever."

She was right.

# FIVE

# A Secret from Mamá

Mamá did well at the music store. When she played and sang songs like *"Cielito Lindo,"* the notes danced through the mall. She was popular with the customers and soon began giving lessons. We were able to feed coins to Jamón again.

Mamá continued her letters to Uncle César, telling him how hard we worked, how honest and thrifty we were, how healthy, how handsome. We always tried, at least in front of Mamá, to earn a good report, although we knew her letters contained no bad ones.

"Pablo is the high school's star basketball player." Mamá did not tell about his broken nose.

"Rosa's songs on the guitar won first prize at the junior-high talent show." No mention of Mamá's patient lessons, nor of their squabbles over practicing.

"Pepe was runner-up in the all-county spelling contest." Not a word about the day I cut school to go skateboarding.

Although Jamón was fed often, we still had not saved enough for fare to Mexico. Mamá needed fillings in her teeth. Mortgage interest rates rose. Food prices went up. So did the price of shoes.

One day after school Rosa made fresh *tortillas* and salsa for our afternoon snack. "Mamá has been trying to save for years now, but we still end up with very little. We will never get to visit Uncle César."

"Who cares?" said Pablo.

"We need to go," said Rosa. "Otherwise Tío will never forgive Mamá. That's why he never writes.

"He should get to know us. He must be lonely, living all by himself on his golden mountain." She grinned. "And don't forget. He needs a family to leave his money to."

"If he has any," grunted Pablo.

I turned to my brother. "What do you mean?"

"You really believe all Mamá's stories?"

"I'd *like* to think that they're true," said Rosa. "But there's only one way to find out."

"Mamá wouldn't lie," I said. That's when I told them my idea.

At first they laughed. Then Rosa said, "The sombrero, Pepe? Why not?"

In Pablo's closet was a sombrero Papá had worn for las fiestas. It was of soft felt, embroidered with gold and silver threads.

Each week we earned money in any way we could. Pablo got a second paper route. Rosa baby-sat. I washed windows and collected cans and bottles. Every Friday we counted our money on Pablo's bed. We hid most of it in the sombrero.

Once a month Pablo emptied the sombrero into a sack like Mamá's, one for American Savings deposits. He made sure Mamá did not run into him at the bank. This was our secret, a secret from Mamá.

• • •

More letters. "Pablo and Rosa were confirmed in the church. They are true soldiers of Christ. Rosa looked beautiful wearing the same dress I wore at my confirmation." "Pablo has a job in a fast-food restaurant. Pepe has taken over his brother's paper routes." "Rosa is selling magazines door-to-door. She won a prize for the most subscriptions."

In her letters Mamá never mentioned her school-work, nor, at last, her graduation from college. Mrs. Salmacia at the store gave her a party and a raise. She let Mamá work half days so she could finish her practice teaching.

With our new jobs, the sombrero filled with dollars fast. Mamá's pig also grew heavy; she made frequent trips to the bank. Pablo would tease her. "Shall we start packing for our trip to Uncle César?"

"Not yet, *chico*."

"But *Mamacita*, you are probably the bank's best customer."

Mamá gave him a solemn look. "Ah, but we have

property taxes to pay. And the insurance is due."

There were always necessities for the house. A washer-dryer. A lawn mower. And some things not so necessary, like a computer and new color TV.

Each time Mamá said "Not yet," with her excuse, Pablo would wink at Rosa and me. We all knew it would not be long.

## SIX
# *SHHH!* BIRTHDAY PLANS

The week before Mamá's birthday we held many private meetings. We were planning a surprise party. And what a *sorpresa*!

Mamá always forgot her own cumpleaños—or pretended to. This year we did not remind her.

"Pepe, you can help me make pork tamales," said Rosa. "That's Mamá's favorite."

"I've ordered a cake from the bakery," said Pablo. "Chocolate." Then, with a sly smirk, he told us about the picture to be drawn in icing on the cake. The picture was part of the surprise.

Pablo was also in charge of decorations, which were the best part of the secret—the best part of the whole fiesta.

On the day of the party, we hurried home from school to get ready. We had invited Mamá's friends from the music store. Mrs. Salmacia would drive her home after work.

Rosa and I raced the kitchen clock to get the tamales wrapped and boiled and the table set with flowers and candles. There was no time to help Pablo with the decorations, which were the most work of all.

Every now and then we peeked into the dining room to watch Pablo on the stepladder. We could not keep from laughing. It was such a perfect sorpresa!

## SEVEN
# THE BIRTHDAY SURPRISE

Shortly before six o'clock Mamá's friends arrived. They gasped when they saw our decorations. We heard them chuckling as they hid in the kitchen.

In our too-tight best clothes we stood by the front door, waiting for the sound of Mamá's key in the lock.

The door opened. We all shouted "¡Sorpresa!" Rosa played *"Las Mañanitas"** on the guitar. We sang the Mexican birthday song as Mrs. Salmacia followed Mamá into the house.

Mamá's eyes grew big. She caught her breath, and could say nothing but, "Oh! Oh, hijos!" Turning pale, she sank into her chair and closed her eyes.

*The traditional birthday song in Mexico

She opened them again and blinked. The dining-room ceiling was strung with crisp dollar bills, hundreds of them.

"Oh, my dear hijos, what have you done?"

"Don't worry, Mamá," said Pablo. "We didn't rob a bank."

## EIGHT
# MAMÁ'S SECRET

All through dinner Mamá sat with a dazed look on her face. "The tamales are delicious," she said, but barely touched them. And when she saw the birthday cake, Mamá started to cry. For there, drawn in white icing over chocolate, was a picture of Uncle César—sombrero, beard, and all.

"Now you have no excuses," said Pablo. "There are enough dollars here to buy four plane tickets to Guadalajara."

Mamá began sobbing. "But my dear hijos, you do not understand."

Rosa said, "Uncle César would welcome us, wouldn't he?"

"Of course," said Mamá, "but . . ."

"We can all go in June," I said, "when school is out. You have vacation coming, Mamá."

"I will allow you an extra week," said Mrs. Salmacia.

"No, no. We cannot," Mamá insisted, her voice shaking. "My dear hijos, I love your kindness, but we cannot . . ."

"We've waited all these years," said Rosa. "We *have* to meet Uncle César. He is our patrón! We want to see his grand hacienda. We want to see Guadalajara."

"You won't find him in Guadalajara," said Mamá. She hid her eyes in her napkin; her body heaved with silent sobs. "He is no longer there."

"So?" said Pablo. He crossed his arms. "Just where has your tío gone?"

Mamá blessed herself and bowed her head. "Uncle César is *con Dios*."

# NINE
# THE PATRÓN

The guests left the party, saying Mamá needed to be alone with us. Mamá said she would bring cake and ice cream to the music store *mañana*.

She sat in her flowered chair. Pablo and I sat on each arm, Rosa on the footstool at her feet.

"How many years," asked Rosa, "has Uncle César been dead?"

Mamá dabbed her eyes. "He passed away many years ago. When Pepe was very small."

"Mamá," said Pablo, "why did you lie to us?"

Mamá looked shocked. "Lie?"

"You wrote letters every week to Uncle César."

"I did not say I mailed them."

"When we did well," said Rosa, "you pretended he would be pleased."

Mamá sat up straight and looked Rosa in the eye. "I'm quite sure that from over my shoulder, Uncle César has been reading every word. And that he's very pleased."

Pablo shook his head. "You said he'd send bushel baskets of money, that he'd take care of us."

Mamá pointed to the strings of dollar bills. "Look, right here? Isn't that a bushel basket of money?"

"But we earned it," said Pablo. "We earned every penny."

"So you did, hijos. I'm proud of you; I'm sure Uncle César is, too." She smiled up at Pablo. "You wouldn't expect him to do *all* the work."

"Shoot," said Pablo. He yanked down a string of bills and left the room.

"The candles you lit were for his *spirit*," said Rosa. "Why didn't you tell us he was with God?"

Mamá leaned down and put her arms around Rosa. "Because, queridos, you had no father. Only your patrón, your protector. I did not want you to be afraid."

"But what about you, Mamá?" I asked. "Weren't you afraid?"

"Oh, Pepe, many times. So very afraid!"

Then she broke into tears again.

# TEN

# UNCLE CÉSAR'S HACIENDA

That summer we took our long-awaited flight to Guadalajara. From the airport we took a rattly bus to the hotel; Mamá did not want to splurge on a taxi.

At the hotel, Mamá took a long time bathing and changing clothes, then insisted we eat lunch before our trip to the hacienda.

"But, Mamá," said Rosa. "Aren't you anxious to get there, to see your old home?"

"More anxious than you can imagine."

After lunch, despite Mamá's protests, Pablo hailed a taxi, which dropped us in front of Hacienda Gonzales. The great house on the golden mountain looked like the one in the picture. But

41

rows of cars were parked in the fields and dozens of people strolled up the tree-lined path to the covered porch.

On the front gate posts were signs, *EL PARQUE DE LA HACIENDA*. An arrow pointing to the house said, *EL MUSÉO*.

"Mamá!" said Pablo. "This isn't a ranch. It's a park!"

"And a museum," said Rosa.

Mamá nodded. "It is not the same as before. But still magnificent, no? *Está bien*; now so many people can enjoy our hacienda."

We passed the fountain and climbed the steps to the spot where Uncle César had posed for his picture. Mamá was several steps below us, gazing up at the dome over the entrance.

"A museum," said Pablo, shaking his head. "I knew it! There never *was* an Uncle César."

Rosa peeked into the enormous entry hall. "I think there probably was one. But I'll bet he didn't live *here*."

At the door of the hacienda there was a rack of

souvenir postcards. Some were photos of Señor Gonzales, much like the one on our mantel. Pablo thumbed through the postcards and shrugged.

When Mamá caught up with us, she put some pesos in a jar that said DONACIÓNES. Her hand shook as the guide handed her a leaflet. "I want to wait," she said. She sounded short of breath. "I want to wait a few minutes before I show you my home."

She sat on a stone bench on the porch and opened the pamphlet, which told about the life of César Gonzales, the hero of Santa María village. She read it to us.

He had begun with a small patch of hillside land, which he cultivated from dawn until dusk. He grew alfalfa and corn for the ranch he would one day own. Little by little he acquired land and built his herd. Because his cattle were so well fed, they became prize stock.

By managing the ranch wisely and training his workers well, César became wealthy even before gold was discovered in the Montaña de Oro.

"The mountain of gold," said Rosa. "Mamá, you've told us that story a million times."

Pablo whispered to me, "I think Mamá read about César in a book."

My stomach felt funny. Could our mamá have told such whopping lies?

The story went on about the church Uncle César built for the village, the free medical clinic he founded, how he donated his surplus crops to the poor.

Mamá sighed, "How could anyone live up to such a patrón?" She closed the folder.

Rosa took it from her and read: "After years of prosperity, Señor Gonzales was visited by bad fortune. His ranch was ravaged by drought and disease; his mines failed to produce. He died a poor man. The state confiscated his lands for taxes."

"A poor man?" said Rosa. "Mamá, you've never told us *this* part of the story."

"What good is bad news to anyone?" Mamá rose from the bench. "César was our patrón."

A guide was leading people through the hacienda. Mamá bypassed the group, saying, "No need to pay extra. I know every inch of this place."

The rooms, with their tiled floors and thick adobe walls, were cool and restful. The walls were draped with rich loomed tapestries. The heavy oak furniture smelled of wax.

Signs that began with POR FAVOR asked the tourists not to touch the vases and candlesticks and not to sit on the richly upholstered chairs and sofas.

At the top of the staircase Mamá entered a large room with a stone fireplace and a curtained four-poster bed. "Ah," she sighed, "It is just the same!" Ignoring the sign, she rushed to the bed and sat on it. "This was my bedroom," she said.

"But, Mamá . . . ," said Rosa.

"It is exactly as I left it on the day I was married."

Rosa looked around. "But, Mamá. Where is the shelf of dolls?"

"I was old enough to marry. What did I need with dolls?"

Rosa frowned. Pablo rolled his eyes. They had already read the sign, *LA RECÁMARA*. "The Bedroom of Señor Gonzales."

# ELEVEN
# MAMÁ'S TOUR

Mamá rose from the bed and began scurrying through the rooms. Her eyes were bright and her cheeks had spots of color. "Come, hijos. Come see los baños." She peeked into several rooms, as if she were lost. "Ah, here we are." The bath displayed fancy mirrors and an onyx tub with gold faucets. It was deep enough to swim in.

She hustled down the hall. "And here is the library, where I learned how to read." The walls were lined with leather-bound volumes that looked as if they had never been touched.

Mamá dashed ahead, returning to the staircase. "But you must see my favorite room, the kitchen, where Miguel the chef taught me to cook."

We followed her into the kitchen. It had an eight-burn woodstove and a wall full of pottery. But there were large pots hanging from an iron rack.

"And now, the dining hall."

Three wrought-iron candelabra hung over a polish table, which must have been thirty feet long. We had pra ticed our table manners, imagining that we would one da be eating here. Now a woven cord prevented our pullir out the chairs.

Pablo had his hands in his pockets. Rosa's were clasp behind her back. They did not share Mamá's excitement

Rosa took me aside. "If Mamá has seen Hacienda Go zales before, it was probably on a guided tour."

"But why would she lie?"

"She thought we needed a patrón."

My steps lagged as we followed Mamá back into tl entry hall. Maybe a patrón was important when we we young, just *niñitos*. But not now. Who cared about Unc César and his house and his ranch and his gold? I wante to tell Mamá there was no more need to lie.

"But wait until you see *la sala*," she said. "I am savir that for last."

# TWELVE
# A BUSHEL BASKET OF MONEY

Mamá crossed the front hall, passing César Gonzales's private chapel. She entered a high-ceilinged room that ran from the front to the back of the house. The walls were paneled, and the fireplace opening was taller than a man. Immense windows looked out to the whole countryside.

"This is where we held our dances," she said.

"The party for my confirmation. And the reception for my wedding."

Mamá's gaze grew dreamy. She did not notice Pablo yawning. Or Rosa fidgeting with a strand of hair.

The tour guide led his group into the room. Mamá became quiet. She was listening to the man tell about the grand fiestas in Hacienda Gonzales. I hoped she would not rush up and join in with her stories. I wished we could leave.

The guide pointed to a painting above the mantel. It was an oil portrait of a large man with a dark beard. He was dressed in an embroidered suit and held a black sombrero at his waist.

By his side was a graceful young woman in a lace dress. She wore a crown of gardenias. Her eyes were deep and shadowy.

"Mamá!" whispered Rosa. "My dress!"

Mamá smiled and crossed her hands, like the girl in the picture.

"The dress I wore for confirmation!"

Mamá nodded but said nothing.

Pablo stared at the picture, his mouth agape. Then, with a sheepish grin, he put his arm around Mamá.

The guide pointed to the picture. "This is César Gonzales and a niece to whom he was very

devoted. No one knows what became of her."

Mamá closed her eyes to hide her tears. She turned toward the door. "Come, hijos, let me show you the chapel."

•   •   •

The chapel was dark except for the glow of vigil lights. Above the altar colored rays streamed from a stained-glass window of the Sacred Heart.

We lit four candles for Uncle César. When my turn came, I thanked him for the bushel basket of money.

I looked over at Mamá, muy hermosa in her silver comb, her silk scarf, and a thrift-shop suit.

Then I reached for another candle.

# Glossary

**roz con pollo** . . . . . . . . . . . . . . . .chicken with rice
  (a-ROSE con POY-o)

**ños** (BA-nyos) . . . . . . . . . . . . . . . .bathrooms

**bé** (beh-BAY) . . . . . . . . . . . . . . . .Baby Jesus

**enas noches** . . . . . . . . . . . . . . . .good night
  (BWE-nas NO-chess)

**rritos de frijoles** . . . . . . . . . . . .bean burritos; a burrito is a tortilla
  (bur-REE-tos day free-HO-lays)   wrapped around a filling

**fé con leche** . . . . . . . . . . . . . . . . .coffee with milk
  (ca-FAY con LEH-chay)

**rne asada** . . . . . . . . . . . . . . . . . .roasted or broiled meat
  (CAR-nay a-SAH-tha)

**ico** (CHEE-co) . . . . . . . . . . . . . . .child, young person

**ilis** (CHEE-lays) . . . . . . . . . . . . . .chiles

**ielito Lindo"** . . . . . . . . . . . . . . . .Mexican love song
  (see-eh-LEE-to LEEN-do)

**mida del Rey** . . . . . . . . . . . . . . . .dinner of the King
  (co-MEE-tha del RAY)

**n Dios** (con DEE-os) . . . . . . . . . .with God

**artos** (KWAR-tos) . . . . . . . . . . . .bedrooms

**mpleaños** . . . . . . . . . . . . . . . . . .birthday
  (coom-play-AH-nyos)

**nero** (dee-NARE-ro) . . . . . . . . . .money

**naciónes** (doh-nas-YON-ehs) . . .donations

55

**el muséo** (el moo-SAY-o) . . . . . . . .the museum
**el parque** (el PAR-kay) . . . . . . . . . .the park
**enchiladas**. . . . . . . . . . . . . . . . . . . . tortillas filled with cheese or meat,
   (en-chee-LA-thas)                   rolled, and covered with sauce
**Esta bién** (es-STA bee-EN) . . . . . . .It's good, fine
**Estados Unidos** . . . . . . . . . . . . . . .United States
   (eh-STAH-thos oo-NEE-thos)
**fiesta** (fee-EH-sta) . . . . . . . . . . . . . .feast, party
**fiesta de cumpleaños** . . . . . . . . .birthday party
  (fee-EH-sta day coom-play-AH-nyos)
**gracias** (GRA-see-us) . . . . . . . . . . . .thank you
**gringo** (GREEN-go) . . . . . . . . . . . . .Yankee, man from the USA
**hacienda** (ah-see-EN-da) . . . . . . . .country house, farm
**Jamón** (ha-MONE) . . . . . . . . . . . . . .Ham
**la Misa del Gallo** . . . . . . . . . . . . . .the Rooster's Mass (see footnote, p. 23)
   (la MEE-sa del GUY-o)
**la recámara** . . . . . . . . . . . . . . . . . .the bedroom
   (la ray-CAH-ma-ra)
**la sala** (la SAH-la) . . . . . . . . . . . . . .the living room, parlor
**"Las Mañanitas"** . . . . . . . . . . . . . .traditional Mexican birthday song
   (las mah-nya-NEE-tas)
**las muñecas** . . . . . . . . . . . . . . . . . .the dolls
   (las moo-NYAY-cas)
**"Las Posadas"** . . . . . . . . . . . . . . . .a song about Mary and Joseph's
   (las po-SAH-thas)                 search for lodging
**la Virgen de Guadalupe** . . . . . . . .the Virgin of Guadalupe,
                                      an important religious figure
   (la VEER-hen day GWA-tha-LOO-pay)
**Mamacita** (ma-ma-SEE-ta) . . . . . . .Little Mamá, a term of affection
**mañana** (ma-NYA-na) . . . . . . . . . . .tomorrow
**mariachis** (ma-ree-AH-chees) . . . .Mexican street musicians
**mi novio** (mee NO-vee-o) . . . . . . . .my sweetheart
**mis hijos** (mees EE-hos) . . . . . . . . .my sons, my children
**Montaña de Oro** . . . . . . . . . . . . . .mountain of Gold
   (mon-TAH-nya day OR-ro)
**muy feliz** (moy feh-LEEZ) . . . . . . . .very happy
**muy hermosa** . . . . . . . . . . . . . . . . .very beautiful
   (moy er-MOH-sa)
**Navidad** (na-vee-THAD) . . . . . . . . .Christmas
**niñitos** (neen-YEE-tos) . . . . . . . . . .little children
**patrón** (pa-TRONE) . . . . . . . . . . . . .patron, protector, hero

**piñata** (pen-YA-ta) . . . . . . . . . . . . . .a papier mâché figuredecrated
                                                 with shredded tissue paper
                                                 and filled with gifts or sweets
**por favor** (pore  fah-VOR) . . . . . . . .please
**querida, querido** . . . . . . . . . . . . . . .dear one, beloved
  (care-REE-tha, care-REE-tho)
**salsa** (SAL-sa) . . . . . . . . . . . . . . . . .salsa, sauce
**sí** (SEE) . . . . . . . . . . . . . . . . . . . . . . .yes
**sombrero** (sum-BRER-ro) . . . . . . . .broad-brimmed hat
**sorpresa** (sore-PRAY-sa) . . . . . . . . .surprise
**tamales** (ta-MAH-lays) . . . . . . . . . . .ground or shredded meat rolled  in
                                                 cornmeal dough, wrapped in husks
                                                 and steamed
**tío** (TEE-o) . . . . . . . . . . . . . . . . . . . .uncle
**tomatillos** (toe-ma-TEE-yos) . . . . . .small fruits resembling green toma-
oes
**tortillas** (tor-TEE-yas) . . . . . . . . . . . .round flat breads of flour or cornmeal